Pinky's First Spring Day

By Amye Rosenberg

A GOLDEN BOOK • NEW YORK

Western Publishing Company, Inc., Racine, Wisconsin 53404

Library of Congress Catalog Card Number : 88-50814   ISBN: 0-307-80160-8

MCMXC

Spring came suddenly to the meadow at the edge of the wood. The sun warmed the earth. The bushes burst with new leaves and juicy berries. The air was sweet with flowers.

Little Pinky hopped onto the soft green grass. He wiggled his little pink nose. This was his first spring day. He and the rest of the Rabbit family were very excited.

"Let us have a celebration," said Mother Rabbit.

"We can spend the day gathering flowers and tender greens," said Father Rabbit.

"We can pick berries!" said the brother and sister rabbits.

"Then tonight," said Uncle Rabbit, "we will feast under the moon and stars!"

So the Rabbit family set off with baskets and sacks to fill with goodies.

Pinky wandered off by himself. Everything looked new to him. He saw a bird for the very first time. It flew from bush to bush.

"That looks like fun!" thought Pinky.

Pinky climbed a low branch. He flapped like a bird. He leapt into the air, expecting to fly. But he crashed in the prickly bushes instead. Ouch!

Then Pinky heard a buzzing noise. It came from a tree that was dripping with something golden and sticky. Pinky tasted sweet honey for the very first time.

"Leave that alone!" buzzed an angry bee, and it stung Pinky right on the nose!

Poor Pinky decided to stay away from bees and honey. He began to gather some flowers instead. He picked yellow, purple, and white ones. Then he saw a frog leap by for the very first time.

Boing! The frog jumped.

Pinky followed the frog. Every time it jumped, he jumped.

Boing! Pinky followed the frog right—splat!—into a mud hole.

Pinky was all covered with mud. So were
his beautiful flowers. He looked for a place to
wash and saw a turtle for the very first time.
She was sunning on a rock near the pond. But
then the turtle dived into the water.

"That will clean me off!" thought Pinky. So he dived off the rock, too.

Splash! Pinky hit the water and sank. It was his very first time in a pond. He hadn't learned to swim yet.

"Help!" Pinky cried.

The turtle, who was gliding through the water, heard Pinky's cries. She swam beneath the sinking bunny.

Pinky was brought safely to shore on the turtle's broad green back.

"Don't ever dive into the water alone!" she warned.

It was getting late. Pinky heard his mother call, "Time to go!"

The soggy little bunny joined the rest of the Rabbit family. They set off for home with armloads of flowers, baskets of berries, and sacks brimming with tender greens.

That night the moon shone splendidly. The stars lit up the sky. The Rabbit family gathered for a grand feast in the meadow at the edge of the wood.

"Pinky!" called Mother Rabbit. "Come wear this necklace of flowers!"

"Pinky!" called Father Rabbit. "Come eat some ripe red berries!"

"Pinky!" called the other rabbits. "Come count the stars!"